ROSIE WOODS

in Jack and the Bean Shock

written by Maya Myers

illustrated by Eleanor Howell

raintree

a Capstone company — publishers for children

For Marilyn and Christine,
the classroom dream team
– MM

Raintree is an imprint of Capstone Global Library Limited, a company incorporated in England and Wales having its registered office at 264 Banbury Road, Oxford, OX2 7DY – Registered company number: 6695582

www.raintree.co.uk
myorders@raintree.co.uk

Designed by Sarah Bennett
Printed and bound in India

978 1 3982 5660 6

British Library Cataloguing in Publication Data
A full catalogue record for this book is available from the British Library.

Contents

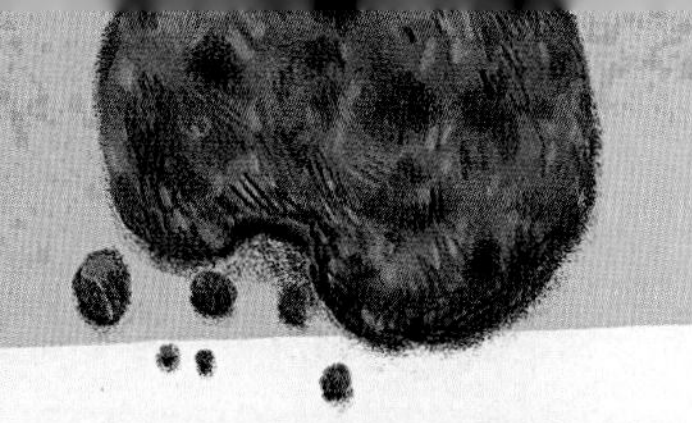

FUN FACTS

ABOUT ME, ROSIE WOODS

1. I love to write in my trusty red notebook.
2. I am quiet. My friend Wolfie is . . . not.
3. I live with my dad, and I can walk to my grandma's house.
4. My teacher, Mrs Marshall, is the GOAT (greatest of all time)!
5. The story you are about to read happened in our classroom.

Chapter One

Beans, beans

"And to learn more about the scientific method, friends, we will be growing . . . BEANS!" Mrs Marshall threw her arms up in the air. She looked like she expected a round of applause, but the whole class just stared at her.

Beans didn't sound too exciting to Rosie. In fact, they were one of her least favourite foods. Green beans? No, thanks. Black beans? Yuck. Kidney beans? NEVER.

In the absence of applause from her pupils, Mrs Marshall clapped her own hands three times.

"That's right, class – BEANS! You are going to design an experiment using the scientific method to learn about beans."

Rosie turned her eyes to her trusty red notebook. She had been taking notes about the steps of the scientific method.

THE SCIENTIFIC METHOD

1. Ask a question

   What happens if ___? Why? How? How much?

2. Research

   Find out more about the thing your question is about.

3. Form a hypothesis (say hi-POTH-uh-sis)

   Make a guess about what will happen.

4. Conduct an experiment

   Do the same thing in different ways.

5. Record the data

   Write down what happens. Take measurements!

6. Draw a conclusion

   Work out if your guess was right.

7. Share the results

   Make a poster! ☺

The first thing was to ask a question. What kind of question could Rosie ask about beans? *Why are beans so slimy? Why do parents make children eat beans? What even is the point of beans?*

"A bean is a seed," Mrs Marshall said. "Seeds grow into plants. Your questions should have something to do with what bean seeds need in order to become the most giant beanstalk of all!"

Phew! Rosie thought. Maybe they wouldn't actually have to eat the beans.

"Your experiment should have at least four different test subjects. Everything should be the same for all four plants, except for one thing. Your group will decide what that different thing will be."

"What groups?" Wolfie called out without raising his hand. "How do we know who's in our group?"

Wolfie was Rosie's good friend, though he did wear her out sometimes with all his talking. It seemed like he never had a thought he didn't say out loud.

"You will be working in table groups for this project," Mrs Marshall said.

"Yes!" Wolfie gave Rosie a high five. "We'll grow the giantest beanstalk of all!"

Rosie gave him a double eyebrow raise. Then she looked across the table at Jack. Jack was writing in his notebook.

Rosie and Wolfie had been sitting at the same table all year, the Harp Table. It was in between the Guitar Table and the Trumpet Table. The Harp Table was right by the window, so it was always sunny and warm there, just the way Rosie liked it. And it had been just Rosie and Wolfie there – until today. Jack was new to their class, and he was very quiet. When Mrs Marshall had brought Jack to their table that morning, he hadn't said hi or anything. He'd just sat down, opened up his notebook and started writing.

In fact, Rosie hadn't heard Jack say a single word yet.

Wolfie never met a person he didn't want to talk to. But Rosie was quiet. She liked quiet things. She didn't always feel like talking, especially to someone new. She guessed Jack might be feeling shy. Rosie thought that if *she* was new, she'd probably want someone to be nice to her. So she took a deep breath and leaned over to Jack, who was still doodling in his notebook.

"Jack? Mrs Marshall said we're gonna

be in a group."

Jack kept writing. He didn't look up. Rosie turned to Wolfie, but he had gone to sharpen his pencil.

Maybe he didn't hear me, Rosie thought. She tried again, making her voice a little louder. "Uh, hey, Jack? You're going to be in a group with me and Wolfie. For the bean project?"

Jack said nothing. He was still writing. Rosie peeked at his paper.

Huh. So Jack had been listening to

giant beans
Giant Beans
GIANT BEANS

Mrs Marshall. He just wasn't listening to Rosie.

Mrs Marshall continued, "To help you

design the best experiments, we'll be going to the media centre to do some research. And class, let me tell you: you *want* to design the best experiment! The group that grows the tallest bean plant by next Monday will win the Golden Egg for the whole week!"

The Golden Egg was a prize everyone wanted. The table with the Golden Egg was first to line up. They got to read the morning announcements. They got to make special trips to deliver things around the school. They got first choice of classroom chores. And they got to pick the read-aloud book. Every table wanted that egg.

Wolfie dropped into his chair. "Did you hear that? The Golden Egg for a whole week! We've got to grow the tallest

beans!" He tilted his head to see Jack's notebook. "Giant beans? Alright! Golden Egg, here we come!"

Jack kept writing, but now he was nodding, like he agreed with Wolfie. So Jack listened to *Wolfie* too.

Well, this could get interesting, Rosie thought. And she wasn't sure it would be interesting in a good way.

Chapter Two

Research and rescue

In the media centre, the class was supposed to be getting books about plants, so they could find out what beans need in order to grow. Then they would pick a question for their experiment.

Mrs Marshall said they needed non-fiction books, but Rosie decided to take a quick look through her favourite section – chapter books. Ooh, there was her favourite series: Giants of Fairyland! She'd read the first two books twice already, and she'd been waiting for forever for the third one to come out.

She couldn't resist picking up book one again. She'd just reread the first couple of pages . . .

"Hey, Rosie, come on!" Wolfie was waving at her from across the room. "There's no plant books over there!"

Rosie's head popped up. Wolfie already had a huge stack of books, and Jack was right behind him. She stuck the book back on the shelf.

By the time she got to the non-fiction section, all the plant books were gone. Rosie felt her face getting hot. Good thing Wolfie was in her group. He never minded sharing.

Wolfie was already reading. Jack had a book open next to him, but he wasn't reading it. He was writing in his notebook again.

Wolfie held a book out to Rosie before she even asked. "Here," he said. "Mrs Marshall said we need to do research to find out what plants need."

"Thanks. I got distracted." Rosie opened the plant book and started reading. "This says seeds need sunlight, nutrients, air and water to grow."

"Whoa, check this out. This one shows a bean seed growing!" Wolfie said. Then he began to chant, "Beans, beans, good for the heart, the more you eat, the more you –!" until Mrs Marshall came over and placed a hand on his shoulder.

That Wolfie.

Rosie looked over and saw that Jack was still writing. Maybe he was waiting for an invitation. "Jack, do you want to help us do research?"

Jack kept his eyes on his paper, where he was drawing a plant. He didn't answer her.

Rosie elbowed Wolfie and gave him a wide-eyed look, the kind that said, *Why isn't Jack helping?*

"Ow, Rosie! What did you do that for?" Wolfie was never any good at body language.

"Never mind," she said. They didn't need Jack's help anyway.

Wolfie leaned over to look at Rosie's book and said, "Mrs Marshall said we need a question about what beans need to grow."

"Yep," Rosie said. Wolfie had a habit of telling Rosie things she already knew.

"So?" Wolfie said. "What's our question going to be?"

“I suppose it should be about what it says here. Sunlight, nutrients, air and water. But that’s not a question. It’s more like an answer.”

“Ooh, I know, I know!” Wolfie said. “How ’bout *how much* of that stuff they need?”

“Like how much sunlight do the beans need?” Rosie asked.

Wolfie tapped his nose with one finger and pointed at Rosie with his other hand. “Yessss! That’s our question, no question about it! Ha, get it? No *question* about it? What do you think, Jack?”

Jack didn’t raise his head, but he did nod. And he started drawing a sun over his plant. At least he was paying attention. To Wolfie.

Rosie and Wolfie spent the rest of their media centre time taking notes and learning all about plants, but Jack just drew pictures the whole time. It didn’t seem fair that Rosie and Wolfie were doing all the work.

When they got back to the classroom, Rosie marched up to Mrs Marshall.

"Did you learn some helpful plant facts in your research?" Mrs Marshall asked.

"Yes, but . . . well, *Jack* wasn't very helpful." Rosie didn't want to tell tales, but she thought Mrs Marshall would want to know what was going on.

Mrs Marshall raised her eyebrows. "Well, Rosie, you know everyone works in their own way. This is Jack's first day with us. It may take some time to get to know his way of working. Let's give him a chance to settle in, okay?"

"Okay," said Rosie. But what if Jack's way of working was not working at all?

Chapter Three

Hippopotamusly speaking

When Rosie got back to the Harp Table, it had a big pile of supplies in the middle of it: a bucket of soil with a spoon in it, small glass jars, marker pens, flat wooden sticks with a pointy end, a little watering can and, of course, bean seeds. This was going to be fun! But before they could touch anything, Mrs Marshall said they needed to write down their question and form their hypothesis. A hypothesis is the guess you make about what will happen in a science experiment.

Rosie got her trusty red notebook and wrote down the question they'd decided on:

How much sunlight makes a bean plant grow the tallest?

She checked with Wolfie to make sure they'd both written the same thing. She leaned over to check Jack's notebook. Rosie didn't know what she might find, but in the middle of the page, there it was:

How much sunlight makes a bean plant grow the tallest?
GIANT BEANS GIANT BEANS

"Okay," Wolfie said, "now we just need a hippopotamus."

Rosie laughed. "What for?"

"You know, like it says in Step 3: Form a hippopotamus."

Rosie shook her head, smiling. *That Wolfie*. "You mean a hypothesis?"

"Yeah, that's what I said," Wolfie said. "It's like a guess, right?"

"Right," Rosie said. "What's our guess?"

"Well, the books said plants need light to grow," Wolfie said. "So my guess is the one with the most light will grow the tallest."

"Yeah, me too," Rosie said. "Jack, what do you think?"

No answer. Jack was still hunched over his notebook.

"Okay, then," Rosie said. "Our hypothesis is: the plant with the most sunlight will grow the tallest." She wrote it down, and so did Wolfie. When she sneaked a glance at Jack's notebook, he was drawing a hippopotamus.

Before the kids were allowed to get their hands dirty planting seeds, Mrs Marshall showed them how to fill the jars with soil, leaving room for water on top. She showed them how to poke holes for the seeds at the side of the jar, so they could see when the roots started growing. She said to put two seeds in each jar, and to water them just enough to get the soil wet each day. Rosie wrote down all the steps.

By the time she had finished her notes, Jack was already spooning soil into the jars. Now that it was getting fun, maybe he'd start being helpful.

Rosie took the watering can to the sink to fill it up. When she came back, she saw that Wolfie had spread all the bean seeds out on the table. He looked like he was counting them. Then, for no reason Rosie could see, he started throwing some out of the open window.

"Wolfie!" she shouted. Everyone – even Jack – was staring, so she lowered her voice. "Don't – what are you *doing*?"

"Shhh!" Wolfie put his finger to his lips and whispered, "I'm getting rid of the bad seeds."

Rosie leaned in and whispered back, "What do you mean 'bad seeds'?"

"In one of the books, it said to only plant bean seeds that look fat and smooth. Those ones were wrinkly."

"Oh. Okay." Rosie sat down. "So why are we whispering?"

"It's our secret weapon. If we only plant the good ones, we'll win the Golden Egg."

Rosie gave Wolfie two thumbs up. She wanted to win.

Wolfie put two fat, smooth beans in front of Rosie, and two in front of Jack. "Two beans in each jar, Mrs Marshall said. So we've got two chances in case one doesn't grow."

Jack had all the jars on his side of the table. He wasn't passing them round.

"Jack?" Rosie asked. "Could I have one of the jars, please?"

Jack didn't move, but Wolfie didn't wait. He just grabbed one and said, "Thanks!"

Rosie waited another few seconds, then she took one too.

Jack still had two jars, so Wolfie gave him two more seeds. "You can do two jars," Wolfie said.

After they'd put the seeds in, they passed around the watering can. Just a little water, like Mrs Marshall said – enough to get the soil wet, but not so much that you could see water pooling at the bottom of the jar.

Tomorrow, they would start Step 4: Conduct an experiment.

* * *

On the bus ride home, Wolfie was rattling off lots of different ideas for how they could set up their experiment, but Rosie kept thinking about Jack.

"Jack is very quiet," she said when Wolfie finally stopped talking to take a drink from his water bottle.

"Yeah, so? You're quiet sometimes," Wolfie said.

"Not *that* quiet," Rosie said.

Wolfie shrugged. "Maybe he's shy."

"Maybe," Rosie said. But she had another hypothesis about Jack. Maybe he just didn't like her.

Chapter Four

In a different light

On Tuesday morning, Rosie couldn't wait to check on their seeds. Jack was already at the Harp Table when she got there. He had lined up all the jars in front of him.

"How do they look?" Rosie asked him.

Instead of answering, Jack went to his drawer and started moving things around, like he was searching for something.

Fine, Rosie thought. She looked at the jars herself and was surprised to find tiny white roots already sticking out from the seeds.

"Mrs Marshall!" she called. "Come and look!"

Mrs Marshall bent down for a better view. "A-ha! Class, Rosie has seen our first signs of growth. Anyone else?"

All around the room, kids bent down to examine their bean seeds, and excited shouts popped up from every table.

"Me!"

"Yes!"

"Wow! It's like magic!"

"What's going on?" Wolfie had just come in.

"Roots – already!" said Rosie.

"As you can see, class, our beans are up to the task!" Mrs Marshall said. "Now it's time for us to design our experiments."

Mrs Marshall said they should keep everything the same for all their plants except for one thing. The thing that changed was called a *variable*. Since the Harp Table's question was about how much light the plants needed, light was their variable. They needed to put their jars in four places that each had a different amount of light.

Fortunately, their table was right next to the window.

"The first one goes right here," Wolfie said, and he put one jar on the sunny windowsill.

"Don't forget the stick," Rosie said. The wooden sticks were for labelling their plants. "Hey, where did the sticks go?"

Wolfie nodded at Jack, who was drawing a beanstalk on a stick. He had

drawn beanstalks on all their sticks.

Rosie couldn't believe it. "Jack, we need those sticks to label our plants!"

"It's okay," Wolfie said. "We can write on the other side." He picked one up and wrote a number *1* on the blank side. Then he stuck it in the jar on the windowsill.

Wolfie scanned the room. "Hey, cool," he said. "Nobody else has pictures on their sticks. Now it's easy to tell which jars are ours. Good idea, Jack!"

Jack's eyes flicked up to Wolfie, then quickly back to the sticks, but Rosie caught a hint of a smile.

Maybe I just need to be nicer to Jack, like Wolfie is, she thought. She smiled and said, "Jack, what do you think for the next one? We need a place with light but not right in the sun."

But Jack was back at his notebook again, scribbling over the whole page.

Rosie's eyes said to Wolfie, *Are you seeing this?* Apparently, Wolfie wasn't.

While Jack was drawing, Rosie and Wolfie found places for the other jars. Jar number 2 went on a shelf near the window but not where the sun would be directly on it. They put number 3 next to the door, on the side of the room furthest away from the window. And for number 4, Rosie had a great idea. "Let's put it in the reading nook!"

The reading nook had a blanket over the top to keep it cosy and quiet. If a plant was in there, it wouldn't get much light at all.

Mrs Marshall gave each group blank charts to record their findings. Rosie's handwriting was a lot neater than Wolfie's, so she decided to start filling in the chart. She carefully wrote their names on the first line, but when she got to Jack's, she hesitated.

Jack was still scribbling. He had filled the whole page with black ink, except in the middle, where he'd drawn a plant growing up from the bottom all the way to the top. All around the border, he'd written *MAGIC BEANS*. Jack might not do much else, but he certainly wrote a lot. Maybe recording their findings would be a good job for him.

"Jack?" Rosie asked. "Do you want to fill in our chart?" She turned it towards him and pushed it across the table.

Jack grabbed the paper and started writing so fast that Rosie was sure he'd make mistakes. Oh, well. They could

Group members: Rosie, Wolfie, Jack

Question: How much sunlight will make a bean plant grow the tallest?

Hypothesis: The plant with the most sunlight will grow the tallest.

Variable: Light

Variables	No.1 Bright light	No.2 Some light	No.3 Low light	No.4 Very low light
Day 1 (Tuesday)	Height: Colour: Leaves:	Height: Colour: Leaves:	Height: Colour: Leaves:	Height: Colour: Leaves:
Day 2 (Wednesday)	Height: Colour: Leaves:	Height: Colour: Leaves:	Height: Colour: Leaves:	Height: Colour: Leaves:

always ask Mrs Marshall for another one. But when Jack had finished, Rosie was in for a surprise.

Jack had filled it out perfectly. And Rosie had to admit his handwriting was just as neat as hers.

* * *

As they lined up for lunch, Rosie asked Jack if he wanted to sit with her and Wolfie in the canteen. He didn't answer. When they got there, Jack just stood next to the table until Wolfie patted the seat next to him and said, "Hey, Jack, want to sit with us?"

Jack sat down.

Rosie didn't get it. She was trying to be friendly. Why wouldn't Jack talk to her?

Just before it was time to go home,

Mrs Marshall asked the class to take their plants' first measurements. She said to use their rulers and measure them in centimetres. For things even smaller than a centimetre, she reminded them they could use the < symbol, which means "less than".

Variables	No.1 Bright light	No.2 Some light	No.3 Low light	No.4 Very low light
Day 1 (Tuesday)	Height: 1 cm Colour: white Leaves: none	Height: 1 cm Colour: white Leaves: none	Height: 1 cm Colour: white Leaves: none	Height: <1 cm Colour: white Leaves: none

So far, all four plants were about the same height. But it was only the first day. Rosie was sure their hypothesis about the beans would be right. She just hoped her hypothesis that Jack didn't like her would turn out to be wrong.

Chapter Five

Broken record

On Wednesday, the groups collected their jars to draw pictures of their growing seeds. That was part of how they were going to record data, which was a fancy scientist way of saying that they were writing down what they saw happening in their experiment. They measured the roots, which were getting longer.

"Hey, this is weird," Rosie said, holding up jars 2 and 4 in front of Wolfie. "The reading nook plant has the longest root."

"Wow!" said Wolfie, and Jack looked up at the jars.

"But our hypothesis," Rosie said, "was that the plant with the *most* light would grow the tallest, not the one with the *least* light. What if we were wrong?"

"We don't have to be right!" Wolfie said. "We just have to have the tallest beanstalk!"

Jack pushed his notebook towards Wolfie. The whole page was filled with the words *GIANT BEANS*.

"See?" Wolfie said. "Jack knows what's what!"

At lunch, Jack sat down next to Wolfie without being asked. Rosie being nicer to Jack didn't seem to be making a difference, so she decided to try another variable: gifts. She reached across the table to give Jack one of Gram's not-so-famous golden coin cookies – they had dates and butternut squash and turmeric to make them golden. Jack took a little bite, but when it was time to dump their trays, Rosie saw him throw the rest away. (She couldn't really blame him.) And he still did not say one word to her.

* * *

On Thursday, all the roots were even longer. Rosie went to get plant 4 from the reading nook so they could record its measurements, but she couldn't find it.

She went back to the table. “Wolfie, did you get our reading nook plant already?”

“No, uh-uh. You said you were going to get it.”

“I did, but it isn’t there. Jack, have you brought number 4 out already?”

Jack didn’t answer. He was measuring roots. But there were only three plants on the table.

Rosie threw up her hands. “Where is plant 4?”

“Beats me,” said Wolfie.

Rosie found Mrs Marshall. “Somebody from another table has taken our plant out of the reading nook.”

“Are you sure about that?” Mrs Marshall asked.

“Well, it’s not there. Someone must have taken it.”

"Hmm," Mrs Marshall said. "Why don't you look around and see if you can find it?"

Rosie searched. She checked on the Trumpet Table and under the Trumpet Table. Then the Piano Table, the Clarinet Table, the Guitar Table and the Violin Table. She climbed on chairs to check the highest shelves and got down on her hands and knees to check the floor. She asked everyone if they'd seen it, but no one had. The Harp Table's plant number 4, with the beanstalk drawn on the stick, had gone.

"What are we going to do?" Rosie asked Wolfie. "It's too late to start a new one. It would never catch up."

Wolfie shrugged. "Dunno. Guess we'll just use three. Don't worry, we still have that big boy in the window."

Rosie put her hands on her hips. "Who says it's a boy?"

"Boy, girl, who cares?" Wolfie said. "It's even started turning green!"

Wolfie was right: the curved top of a green stem was poking out above the soil.

"Yep, number 1 is our winner," Wolfie assured her. "The Golden Egg will be OURS!" He cackled like an evil genius.

But Rosie didn't feel like laughing.

Variables	No.1 Bright light	No.2 Some light	No.3 Low light	No.4 Very low light
Day 1 (Tuesday)	Height: 1 cm Colour: white Leaves: none	Height: 1 cm Colour: white Leaves: none	Height: 1 cm Colour: white Leaves: none	Height: <1 cm Colour: white Leaves: none
Day 2 (Wednesday)	Height: 3 cm Colour: white Leaves: none	Height: 3 cm Colour: white Leaves: none	Height: 2.5 cm Colour: white Leaves: none	Height: 4 cm Colour: white Leaves: none
Day 3 (Thursday)	Height: 4 cm Colour: green Leaves: none	Height: 4 cm Colour: light green Leaves: none	Height: 3 cm Colour: white Leaves: none	Height: Colour: MISSING Leaves:

Chapter Six

Sprout surprise

By Friday, both the plants in jar 1 had poked all the way out of the soil. Two little green leaves were sticking out from each stem. The tallest stalk was seven centimetres high. The plants in jar 2 and jar 3 had little leaves too, though the ones in 3 were a lighter green colour. So far, there wasn't much difference in the size of the plants.

Unfortunately, plant 4 was still missing.

Out on the playground that afternoon, Leo and Malia asked Rosie to play four square. Since there was room for one more, Rosie asked Jack if he wanted to play too. Jack scuffed his feet on the ground, but she could tell he was thinking about it.

Then Wolfie ran past. "Hey, Jack, come and play football with me, Ali and Declan!"

Jack ran off with Wolfie. *Of course he did,* Rosie thought.

Four square is quite hard to play with only three people, and Rosie kept missing the ball. Once, it bounced past her and rolled all the way over to the building, right under their classroom window. Rosie jogged to get it, glancing over her shoulder at the football game. There was Jack, running and playing with those boys. Why wouldn't he play with her?

As Rosie scooped up the ball, a little green something on top of the soil caught her eye. She bent down.

Bean sprouts! What were beans doing out here? Then Rosie remembered the seeds Wolfie had thrown out the window. Some of Wolfie's "bad beans" had sprouted even without being planted.

"Wolfie! Jack!" Rosie shouted. "Come and see!"

They both came sprinting over.

"Wolfie, I don't think your bad beans were so bad after all," Rosie said, pointing.

"Wait – are those the ones I threw out of the window?" Wolfie dropped to his knees to inspect them. "Cool beans! Ha ha, get it? *Cool beans?*"

Rosie grinned. "Do you think Mrs Marshall will let us use these?"

"I'll ask!" Wolfie said and ran off.

Jack looked around, then picked up a big magnolia leaf shaped like a scoop. He scraped some soil onto it. Then he crouched beside the sprouted beans and reached towards them.

"What are you doing?" Rosie asked. It accidentally came out sounding a bit mean, and Jack dropped the leaf.

Wolfie came running back over. "We can use the bad beans! Mrs Marshall said we can use the bad beans!" He skidded to a halt, sending a spray of soil over the sprouts and Rosie's shoes.

Wolfie looked from Rosie to Jack, then back to Rosie. "What are you guys doing?" But instead of waiting for an answer, he took off again, shouting, "A jar! We need a jar!"

"Sorry," Rosie said to Jack. She really

did want to be his friend. She picked up the leaf and held it out to him.

Jack used the leaf to very gently scoop up the sprouts.

"Hey, good idea," Rosie said, but Jack was already walking towards Wolfie, who was running back with a jar full of soil. Jack tipped the leaf so the sprouted seeds slid into the jar.

"Lucky beans!" Wolfie said. "Now we

have four again!"

Just before the bell rang, Mrs Marshall reminded the class to water their plants. "We'll be away from our beans all weekend, so give them a little extra water – but not too much! We don't want any soggy beans around here."

Wolfie was leaning over Jack's shoulder, laughing at something in Jack's notebook. They didn't seem to be paying attention, so Rosie announced loudly, "I guess I'll water our plants, then."

Neither one of them looked up.

Rosie filled the watering can and visited each plant: 1 in the window, 2 on the shelf, 3 by the door. Then she crawled into the reading nook, where they'd put the new sprouts from outside.

Rosie almost dropped the watering

can. The third book in the Giants of Fairyland series was lying right there on the floor! She had seen Leo reading it this week and had been impatient for him have finished it. He must have finished it today.

Rosie couldn't believe her good luck – and on a Friday, even! She'd have time to read the whole thing over the weekend, if Mrs Marshall would let her borrow it.

Mrs Marshall said yes! Rosie barely had time to tuck the book in her backpack before the bell rang. Yippee, this was going to be a great weekend!

Chapter Seven

Jumping to conclusions

Rosie spent the weekend reading. The new book was even better than the last one. But sometimes her thoughts distracted her. She couldn't stop thinking about how Jack wouldn't play with her or talk to her. When she went to Gram's on Sunday, she told her all about it.

"And I *tried* to be nice, Gram. I even gave him one of your golden coin cookies." Rosie left out the part about Jack throwing it away. "I asked him to play four square, and he just ignored me *again,* and then he ran off to play with Wolfie and some other boys."

"Is that so?" Gram asked.

"Yes. It's not fair. At first I thought he just didn't like *me.*"

Gram nodded slowly. "But now you think . . . ?"

"Well, it's pretty obvious," Rosie said.

Gram cocked her head to the side and waited for Rosie to finish.

"He doesn't like *girls.* I'm going to tell Mrs Marshall."

"Oh?" Gram asked.

"Exactly," Rosie said, crossing her arms.

"Well," Gram said. "I'm sure you know best, my little red Rose."

* * *

Monday morning, Rosie asked Dad to drop her at school a little early. She wanted to be the first one in the classroom. She was feeling nervous as she stepped through the door.

"Good morning, Rosie!" Mrs Marshall said. "I'm so glad you're here. I've been wanting to thank you."

This was a surprise. "What for?"

"You and Wolfie did such a good job of making Jack feel at home during his first week with us. I knew he would need some extra-special friends, which is exactly why I placed him at the Harp Table with you two. You were patient and kind, just like I knew you would be. Oh, I do like it when I'm right." Mrs Marshall clapped for herself, then patted Rosie's shoulder.

"Um, okay," Rosie said. This was not what she had been expecting at all.

"So thank you very much. And I'll tell Wolfie the same when he gets here."

Rosie nodded. "Uh-huh. You're welcome." She took her backpack to her hook but then turned and walked back to Mrs Marshall.

"What can I help you with?" Mrs Marshall asked.

"It's just, well . . . Jack won't talk to me. At all. I tried to be nice, but . . . did I do something wrong?"

Mrs Marshall smiled. "No, Rosie. You did just right. You let Jack be Jack. Different things make different people feel comfortable. You're giving Jack space to discover what makes him comfortable here at our school, and that's exactly what he needs."

Rosie supposed that made sense. Sometimes she needed some time alone in the reading nook. Sometimes Wolfie needed to run a lap around the playground to let out extra energy. Maybe Jack just needed to be quiet. Maybe, Rosie realized, Jack being quiet didn't have anything to do with her at all.

As other kids slowly trickled in to the

classroom, Rosie gave Jack a little wave. "Hi, Jack."

Jack didn't meet her eyes, but he did raise his hand and give a tiny wave back! Maybe he was starting to feel more comfortable, like Mrs Marshall had said. But, then again, Wolfie had already dropped into his seat behind her, so maybe Jack had actually been waving at Wolfie.

Rosie didn't have time to worry about that, though. She put her notebook down on the table and went to check on their plants. They had all grown a lot over the weekend. Just as they'd predicted, the one on the windowsill was flourishing! The stem was tall and green, and two big leaves had spread out to soak up the sunlight.

Wolfie let out a whoop. "Golden Egg, get ready for your trip to the Harp Table! I bet no one has a beanstalk as tall as ours!"

Rosie walked around the room to check out the competition. The Trumpet Table had a pretty tall one, strong and green. As she passed the Guitar Table, Tai and JJ were bumping fists. "We've got twenty centimetres!" Nela called out. "Beat that!"

Rosie hurried back to the Harp Table. "Where's my ruler?"

"I. Am. Your. Ruler," Wolfie said in a deep voice. "Obey my every command."

Rosie rolled her eyes, but she couldn't help laughing. And neither, she was surprised to see, could Jack.

Chapter Eight

Magic beans

The plant in the window was definitely the tallest: eighteen centimetres. It had grown eleven whole centimetres over the weekend! That was amazing, but it wasn't tall enough to beat the Guitar Table's twenty centimetres.

Rosie's shoulders slumped. "Rats."

But Wolfie perked up. "Hey, what about the bad beans?"

"Oh! I'll get 'em!" Rosie said, heading for the reading nook. But when she got there, she stopped short and put her hand over her mouth. There was the jar with the sprouts from the playground, and next to it was the watering can – still half full! Rosie had been so excited about the new Giants of Fairyland book that she had forgotten to water the plant! Without any water, the sprouts had shrivelled up. She had killed them.

Rosie slinked back to the table holding the jar of sad, bad beans. She slumped down in her chair and put her head down on her arms.

"What's the matter?" Wolfie said. "Why do you look so – oh. Uh-oh. What happened?"

Rosie's voice was muffled as she spoke into her arms. "I forgot to water them."

"Oh no, Rosie, that's not good. Plants need water. That's one of the main things it said in the books. And we put that plant in there on Friday. That means it went the whole weekend with no water."

"I *know*, Wolfie!"

Wolfie patted her shoulder. "It's okay, though. We've still got three plants left."

"But they're all shorter than twenty centimetres." Rosie lifted her head. "We're not going to win the Golden Egg."

Then Jack put down his pencil. He went over to the drawers and opened his up. He carefully took something out, then came back to the table.

"Whoa!" Wolfie said. "What is that?"

Jack was holding one of the bean jars, but the plant growing out of it was nothing like the other plants. This was white, with slightly yellowish leaves.

And it was very, very tall!

Rosie checked the stick in the jar. "Hey, it's number 4! That's our missing plant! Jack, you *did* take it!"

Jack drooped, just like the unwatered plants.

"Who *cares* if he took it, Rosie?" Wolfie said. "Look at that beast! It's gotta be the tallest beanstalk in the whole class!"

"It is pretty giant," Rosie admitted, holding her ruler next to it. "Wow . . . *twenty-seven* centimetres! I guess you knew what you were doing, Jack."

Jack flipped the pages of his notebook until he found the one that was coloured all black and had *MAGIC BEANS* written around the edges. He pointed to it.

"Yeah!" Wolfie said. "Cool beans, Mr Magic Beans!" He put up his hand, and Jack gave Wolfie a high five.

"So wait," Rosie said, "the only plant that was completely, totally in the dark grew the tallest of all?"

"Isn't that, like, the opposite of our hippopotamus?" Wolfie asked.

"Yeah," Rosie said, laughing in disbelief.

"Good thing we didn't have to guess right!" Wolfie said. "We just needed . . ." He nodded at Jack, who turned the page in his notebook and held it up.

"GIANT BEANS!" Rosie and Wolfie said together.

Rosie gave Wolfie a double eyebrow raise, and Wolfie gave her a double high five. And then, to Rosie's shock, so did Jack. And though he turned away straight afterwards, Rosie was pretty sure she saw him smile.

Chapter Nine

When wrong is right

As Rosie and Wolfie measured the plants, Jack recorded the data on their chart.

Variables	No.1 Bright light	No.2 Some light	No.3 Low light	No.4 Very low light
Day 1 (Tuesday)	Height: 1 cm Colour: white Leaves: none	Height: 1 cm Colour: white Leaves: none	Height: 1 cm Colour: white Leaves: none	Height: <1 cm Colour: white Leaves: none
Day 2 (Wednesday)	Height: 3 cm Colour: white Leaves: none	Height: 3 cm Colour: white Leaves: none	Height: 2.5 cm Colour: white Leaves: none	Height: 4 cm Colour: white Leaves: none
Day 3 (Thursday)	Height: 4 cm Colour: green Leaves: none	Height: 4 cm Colour: light green Leaves: none	Height: 3 cm Colour: white Leaves: none	Height: Colour: MISSING Leaves:
Day 4 (Friday)	Height: 7 cm Colour: green Leaves: 2	Height: 7 cm Colour: green Leaves: 2	Height: 6 cm Colour: green Leaves: 2	Height: 2 cm (sprouts) Colour: green Leaves: none
Day 7 (Monday)	Height: 18 cm Colour: green Leaves: 2	Height: 16 cm Colour: green Leaves: 2	Height: 17 cm Colour: green Leaves: 2	Height: 27 cm!! Colour: white!! Leaves: 2 (tiny)

Jack's no-light plant was the tallest in the whole class, by a lot. The Harp Table could only draw one conclusion, which was the opposite of their hypothesis: Plants with the least light grow the tallest.

"Hey!" Wolfie said. "Let's put number 4 back in the dark! Maybe if we leave it in there, it will grow as tall as the ceiling! Or the whole school! Even up to the clouds!"

That Wolfie had a giant imagination.

After Jack tucked the plant back into his drawer, Rosie asked another question. "Why?"

Jack walked over to the computer. Rosie and Wolfie followed, and they read over his shoulders as he typed: *Why do plants grow taller in the dark?*

"A-ha," Rosie said. "This says light is so important for plants that if they don't have any, they stretch and stretch to try to find some!"

"I get it," Wolfie said. "It's like if your mum puts the biscuits on top of the fridge, you have to stretch really tall to get them, and sometimes you even have to get on the worktop to get even taller!"

That Wolfie.

Now Rosie thought of another question. "Jack, ask how come they're white instead of green?"

And for the first time ever, Jack did something Rosie had suggested! He was a fast typer too.

Wolfie pulled on his hair. "If you don't stop asking questions, we're going to be doing science forever!"

“What’s so bad about that?” Rosie said.

Wolfie thought for a second. Then he laughed. “Nothing! This is fun! But first let’s go and get that Golden Egg.”

* * *

The Golden Egg glowed in the sunlight at the centre of the Harp Table as Rosie and Wolfie put the finishing touches on the poster that showed the results of their experiment. Jack was writing in his notebook.

Wolfie said, “Yep, looking good! I think we’re done. Did you want to add anything else, Jack?”

Jack held out his notebook. He had drawn three kids with super long legs, who looked just like Rosie and Wolfie

And OF COURSE
you guys could go up the
beanstalk first, so I could catch
you if you – NO, WAIT, it's so I
can catch the golden eggs you
throw down when you find the
MAGIC HEN! Yeah, we're
gonna need a carton for
all our golden eggs!
BEANS

and Jack – well, except for the legs. They had beanstalks twirling all around them. Across the top, it said *GIANT BEANS,* and at the bottom, it said *GIANT FRIENDS*.

"Here's to friends getting things wrong!" Wolfie said, raising the Golden Egg over his head. "Harp Table forever!"

Jack looked at Wolfie, who gave him a fist bump. Then Jack looked at Rosie. His eyes said, *I'm glad we're friends.*

Rosie smiled to say, *Me too.* It was nice to have at least one friend who was good at body language.

And then she laughed, because she realized that her hypothesis about Jack had been wrong too. She'd never thought being wrong could feel so right.

Discussion questions

1. What is a variable? What was the variable in the Harp Table's experiment?

2. Can you think of other variables a group could have used when growing seeds? (Think about all the things a plant needs in order to grow.)

3. If you could design a science experiment about anything, what question would you want to answer? What would your hypothesis be?

4. Did you think it was fair that Rosie felt annoyed when it seemed like Jack wasn't helping the group?

5. What are some things that help you feel comfortable in a new situation? Do your friends have different ways of feeling comfortable?

6. Find the story "Jack and the Beanstalk" in your library or online. How many things can you find in this book that remind you of the original story?

Digging deeper

More about the scientific method

Science is cool! It can be fun to read about science experiments, but it's even more fun to do them yourself. Whenever you want to see science in action, you can use the scientific method. Here are the steps:

1. Ask a question What do you want to know? Can a plant survive without light? Can a biscuit go mouldy? What's the fastest way to melt an ice cube?

2. Research Find out more about whatever your question is about. Look for books in the library. Ask a grown-up to help you search the internet for articles, pictures and videos.

3. Form a hypothesis Make a prediction, or a guess, about what you think will happen. What would make the most sense, based on what you already know?

4. Conduct an experiment Do the same thing in different ways. If you only change one thing in the experiment, and you change that same thing each time, you'll know that's what made the results different. The thing you change is called a variable.

5. Record the data Write down information about what happens in your experiment. This may mean taking measurements, or noticing changes such as colour, shape and size. Drawing pictures or taking photos can help you remember how things change as your experiment goes along.

6. Draw a conclusion Work out whether your hypothesis was correct or not. If it wasn't, think about why. As Rosie discovered, this may lead to more questions, which may lead to more experiments!

7. Share your results Tell a friend or your whole class about what you have learned. You might inspire someone else to try an experiment too!

About the author

photo by Robert Webb

Maya Myers writes books for children and edits books for children and adults. She's a former teacher and loves cooking, gardening and (of course) reading – just like Rosie! Originally from Maine, USA, Maya now lives in North Carolina, where she grows lots of vegetables, including beans, in her garden. She has three children, six chickens and a large cat called Hoss.

About the illustrator

photo by Jayden Campbell Photography

Eleanor Howell is a British writer and illustrator living in Toronto, Canada. She is interested in storytelling in its many forms, and has two master's degrees in Museum Studies and Archiving and is embarking on her third degree, in English Literature. Eleanor loves reading, walking and eating chocolate, but has yet to master the art of doing all three at the same time.